# Yes, Hutoxi!

*story* Radhika Chadha

*pictures* Priya Kuriyan

Tulika

Hutoxi the horse walked around the jungle.
Hmm, there was Mannu the monkey, tossing nuts
into the banana patch.

"Yow! Uff! Aiyyo!!" the little chameleons yelped as
nuts rained down on them.

"Mannu, stop that at once!" snorted Hutoxi.

"Yes, Hutoxi," muttered Mannu.

Ritu the rabbit scurried to the river to drink some water.

Chandu the crocodile floated by, quietly, silently, just like a log of wood.....

..... and suddenly leapt out of the water.

"Yaaaaah!" shrieked Chandu, laughing.

"Eeeeeee!" squeaked Ritu.

"Chandu, stop it! You gave her such a fright!" said Hutoxi sternly.

"Yes, Hutoxi," mumbled Chandu.

Now, what was that rumpus at the mudpit?

Anna and Akka, the elephant teenagers, were playing coconut football.

Anna kicked the coconut and yelled, "GOAL!"

The coconut flew past Akka and — oh no! — landed near the sleeping piglets.

"Anna, Akka, you really should be more careful!" scolded Hutoxi. "You could have hurt the little ones."

"Yes, Hutoxi," grumbled Anna and Akka.

The next day, the animals gathered together.

"Hutoxi's always scolding us," complained Mannu and Chandu.

"We can't have any fun with her around," sulked Anna and Akka.

Just then, Kamini the chameleon came running, turning pink and purple and orange with excitement.

"Is Hutoxi going somewhere?" she asked.
"I saw her leaving the jungle!"

Bahadur the baby elephant ran to the banana patch with Kamini.

"Look, there's Hutoxi," said Kamini to Bahadur. "She's trotting off to Kaligufa Hill."

Kaligufa Hill?! That was at the very edge of the jungle.

Bahadur's mother Amma had told him never to go beyond the banana patch.
So he stopped there and watched Hutoxi.

Where was she going?

Hutoxi reached the top of Kaligufa Hill.
She raised her head and sniffed.
Then she cantered down the hill, away
from the jungle.

"Hutoxiiiii!" yelled Bahadur, alarmed.

But there was no reply.
Hutoxi had disappeared.

Bahadur ran back and told the animals
what he had seen.

"Yaaaaay!" cackled Mannu.

"No more snorts and scolds!" said Chandu.

Anna and Akka danced a happy little jig.

But days passed by and  there was no sign
of Hutoxi.

Bahadur was puzzled and worried.
Why had Hutoxi gone away?

"I'm bored of tossing nuts," said Mannu one day.

Chandu stopped leaping in and out of the water.
"It's no fun," he said.

Anna and Akka didn't enjoy coconut football any more.

Somehow, without Hutoxi, the jungle didn't seem the same.

Amma saw their sad faces and felt sorry for them.
"I'll tell you where Hutoxi is", she said.

"Hutoxi wasn't born in the jungle, you know," said Amma.

"She lived with a herd of wild horses, far away. One day, she got lost. Kamalnayan the camel met her and brought her here.

A few days back we got news that a herd of horses had come near Kaligufa Hill. Hutoxi has gone to meet them. They might be her family."

The animals moped around sadly.
They had become used to Hutoxi's snorts and scolds.
Now they could do whatever they wanted, but it just
wasn't fun.

"What if she never comes back?" sniffed Bahadur,
tearing apart some bananas.

"Bahadur, you untidy little chap! Clear up that
mess!" said a familiar stern voice.

Bahadur jumped up.
"Hutoxi, you're back!" he squealed happily. "I thought you'd gone off with your family."

"Silly fellow, all of you are my family now," said Hutoxi, nuzzling Bahadur fondly.
"Besides, without me what a mess this jungle would be. Wouldn't it?" she asked.

"YES, HUTOXI!" said all the animals, happily.

For Mummy, with much love – *R.C.*
For Sarah, who can now read on her own – *P.K.*

**Other titles in this bestselling series**
*(available in English, Hindi, Tamil, Malayalam, Kannada, Telugu, Marathi, Gujarati, Bangla)*
I'm So Sleepy
Snoring Shanmugam
Colour-Colour Kamini
Mallipoo, Where Are You?

**Yes, Hutoxi! (English)**
ISBN 978-81-8146-769-0
© *text* Radhika Chadha
© *illustrations* Priya Kuriyan
First published in India, 2009
Reprinted in 2012

Published by
Tulika Publishers, 24/1 Ganapathy Colony Third Street, Teynampet, Chennai 600 018, India
*email* tulikabooks@vsnl.com   *website* www.tulikabooks.com

Printed and bound by
Rathna Offset Printers, 40 Peters Road, Royapettah, Chennai 600 014, India

To order books visit www.tulikabooks.com